Hardwick House

Christmas Tree Wood

Four-Leaf Clover Field

River Noodle

Little Red

MDB ~ Thank you, my dearest friend, for your golden soul, your treasured friendship, and for showing me a wonderful new world.   —S. F.

For Jessica. Thank you for your encouragement, enthusiasm, and friendship.   —S. W.

SIMON & SCHUSTER
BOOKS FOR YOUNG READERS
An imprint of Simon & Schuster Children's
Publishing Division
1230 Avenue of the Americas, New York,
New York 10020
Text copyright © 2003 by Sarah,
The Duchess of York
Illustrations copyright © 2003 by
Sam Williams
SIMON & SCHUSTER BOOKS FOR YOUNG
READERS is a trademark of Simon & Schuster.
LITTLE RED is a trademark of Sarah,
The Duchess of York, and is used under license.
Book design by David Bennett
The text for this book is set in Goudy.
The illustrations for this book are rendered in
soft pencil and watercolor on Arches paper.
1 2 3 4 5 6 7 8 9 10

Manufactured in the United States of America
Library of Congress
Cataloging-in-Publication Data
York, Sarah Ferguson, The Duchess of, 1959-
Little Red / Sarah Ferguson, The Duchess
of York ; illustrated by
Sam Williams.— 1st ed.
p. cm.
Summary: While on a picnic with three
friends, a plucky doll named Little Red
decides to investigate a noise that doesn't
sound very friendly.
ISBN 0-689-84340-2 (hardcover)
[1. Dolls—Fiction.
2. Picnicking—Fiction.
3. Animals—Fiction.] I. Williams, Sam, 1955-
ill. II. Title.
PZ7.F35815 Li 2003
[E]—dc21
2002011769
First Edition

Little Red

Sarah Ferguson
The Duchess of York

Illustrated by
Sam Williams

Simon & Schuster Books for Young Readers
New York   London   Toronto   Sydney   Singapore

It was a beautiful sunny day at Buttercup Cottage.
Little Red's cozy home was nestled between the shade of Bluebell
Wood and the Hardwicks' large white house.

Little Red and her friends busily prepared for their picnic at Lily Pad Pond.

They filled their basket to the brim with dandelion tea, sherbert sandwiches, and chocolate cake.

Little Red added a bundle of carrots for Roany the Pony. Gino the Dog was so happy, he sang a growly little song as he helped Little Red pack lunch.

"That's everything," said Little Red as she crossed the last item off of her list.

"What a buzz of a day!" Little Blue was so excited, he couldn't stay still and he skipped around the kitchen.

"Don't forget this!" Little Blue grabbed Little Red's sack of smiles from the table.

"Right! Now we're off!" said Little Red.

Little Red shut the door to the cottage. Roany stood waiting impatiently with the wonky wooden wagon.

"Tosh!" Roany snorted. "I've been waiting for you forever and I'm getting hungry!"

"Oh, Roany, you're always hungry! Not to worry. We're bringing plenty of food. All aboard!" Little Red called.

As the jolly group meandered through the ferns and bluebells on the path to Lily Pad Pond, they sang:

We're going on
a picnic,
a picnic,
a picnic.
We're going on
a picnic!
Isn't it grand?

We're going to feast
on tasty sweets
and run and jump—
it's such a treat
to be going on a picnic!
Isn't it grand?

"What a buzz of a day!" Little Blue shouted.
"Perfect for a picnic!"

Suddenly Roany came to an abrupt stop, nearly making
the wonky wooden wagon topple over.

"What is it, Roany?" Little Red asked.

"I'm famished! Can't I have a carrot or two?" Her belly
rumbled.

"I'm hungry too!" Little Blue piped up. "Let's just have
our picnic right here!"

Little Red felt a little hungry herself. So she swung down from the wagon and opened the picnic basket.

She spread the blanket on the woodland floor and took out her tea set.

"Well, this *is* a nice spot," Little Red said.

Little Red passed out the sherbert sandwiches. Little Blue passed Roany her bunch of carrots. Gino settled down on a corner of the blanket to chew on his sandwich, and his waggly tail created a soft breeze.

The friends munched happily. They basked in the sun, and watched the bees dart in and out of the flowers, and listened to the birds sing in the trees. Suddenly they heard a **dreadful** noise.

SPLAT SHWOOSH THWACK THUMP SQUEAK SPLOSH

"What was that?" whispered Little Red. She quietly slipped on her sack of smiles.

Little Blue tugged on his bumblebee bobble hat. "I think it's time we go home," he said as he trembled just a little. "I don't like it here in the woods anymore. Let's go back to Buttercup Cottage."

"Hold on!" Little Red said. Little Blue jerked backward as Little Red grabbed his straps.

"Don't you think we should see what's going on?"

"Not really," said Roany.

SPLAT SHWOOSH THWACK
THUMP SQUEAK SPLOSH

There was that sound again—and it seemed to be coming from Lily Pad Pond.

Little Blue said shakily, "That noise doesn't sound very friendly."

Little Red took a deep breath. If someone was in trouble, she and her friends should try to help.

SPLAT SHWOOSH THWACK THUMP SQUEAK SPLOSH

"Come on, everyone. I bet it's not as bad as it sounds!" But Little Red wasn't entirely sure.

Little Red squared her shoulders. "That does it," she said in her bravest voice. "I am going to investigate. Anyone care to join me?"

Roany chewed the last bit of carrot in her mouth and said, "Oh, tosh! Let's get this over with so we can enjoy our picnic."

Little Blue shrugged and thought, *If they're going to go, I don't want to be left behind.* And he, too, took a step toward the pond.

The four friends all crept silently toward
the **dreadful** noise.

SPLAT SHWOOSH THWACK
THUMP SQUEAK SPLOSH

They peeked over the trunk of a huge, fallen silver birch
tree. They couldn't believe their eyes!

There—in the middle of the pond—a bunny floated on a lily pad.

An enormous heron shouted orders from the bank to an army of frogs who were trying to tow the stranded bunny to shore.

"Left a bit! Right a bit! Get a move on! Hurry up! Keep going!" he boomed. But no matter how hard the frogs tried, they just weren't strong enough to pull the lily pad with the bunny to safety.

"What a buzz! You sure look like you could use some help!" Little Blue called.

"What can we do?" asked Little Red as she slid down the bank to the pond. Gino followed Little Red to the pond, barking and waggling his tail; he wanted to help too.

"Well, come on then, stop dithering over there, for goodness' sake. Get a move on! Chop, chop!" thundered the heron.

"Oh, please help!" Bunny anxiously called. "I was playing leapfrog with my friends. Why, I can leap farther than any of these frogs." Her pink nose twitched with pride. "But now look what happened! And I can't swim!" Bunny's ears flopped down in despair.

Quickly Little Red reached into her magic sack of smiles—she was sure there was something in there to help. She pulled out a long, sturdy rope.

"Tie one end around my bridle," Roany said. "I'll pull her out of the pond." The pony tossed her head and then muttered, "I sure hope there's a bunch of carrots ready for me when I'm done."

"Stand back!" yelled Little Blue, and all of the frogs hopped to the edge. Roany waded out into the middle of the pond.

When she drew close enough, she tossed the free end of the rope to Bunny. "Hold tight, now!" Roany instructed. Bunny nodded her head, ears bobbing furiously, and she gripped the rope with all her might.

Slowly and very carefully Roany
turned and began to walk back to the
edge of the pond, pulling the bunny
and the lily pad behind her.

A great ripple of cheers rose up. "Fantiddlyfroggytastic!"
croaked the biggest, greenest frog of all. "We thought we
would never get her out!"

"Bravo! Good work, I say!" said the heron as he clapped
his giant wings together.

Little Red and Little Blue ran over to Bunny.

"Are you all right?" they asked.

Bunny laughed. "Of course I'm all right! I'm the champion jumper of the entire woods. I jumped farther than any of those frogs today!" But she paused and then she giggled. "Of course, I jumped so far I couldn't get back by myself!" And the little bunny twitched her nose as her eyes sparkled. "Thank you all for helping me."

"You're lucky you had brave picnickers around like me!" Little Blue said.

Roany groaned.

"Come on, everyone," Little Red said. "Let's all go enjoy our picnic. There's plenty for everyone!"

Everyone sat down to a delicious picnic in Bluebell Wood.

Roany even shared her carrots with Bunny.

And after all had eaten to their heart's content, they passed a perfect afternoon playing leapfrog.

The Village

Sansomes Meadow

Bluebell Wood

Buttercup Cottage

Purdey's Pasture

Lily Pad Pond